To the dancing queen, Patti Ann Harris — S.R.

Library of Congress Cataloging-in-Publication Data available

ISBN 978-0-545-90005-8

10 9 8 7 6 5 4 3 2 1   18 19 20 21 22

Printed in China 38
First edition, May 2018
Book design by Steve Ponzo
Jacket design by Steve Ponzo and Liz Casal

Zoogie Boogie FEVER!

An Animal Dance Book
SUJEAN RIM

Orchard Books • New York
An Imprint of Scholastic Inc.

PSSST. Hey, you! Have you ever wondered why all the animals at the zoo seem so tired?

Did you ever ask yourself why they're all such a bunch of lazybones, lounging around?

**Have you ever wondered what
these animals do at night
. . . after the zoo closes . . .**

when NO ONE is looking?

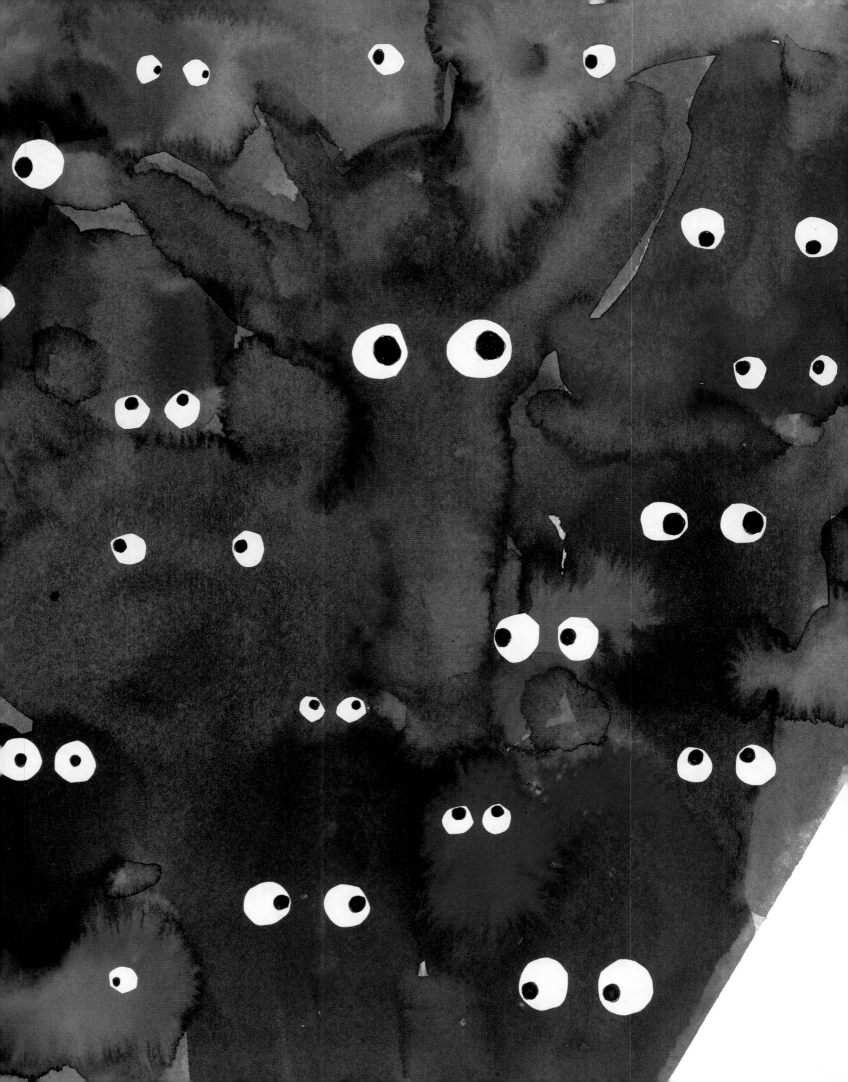

You're not going
to believe it! But I'll show
you. Come with me. Slowly
. . . **TURN THE PAGE** . . .

AND DON'T. TELL. ANYONE.

It all starts with the **GIRAFFES.**
First, they make sure the coast is clear . . .

then they
signal to the
ELEPHANTS,

who cue the
MONKEYS,

who alert
the BIRDS,

who let all
the others know that
it's time. Yes, that's right.

IT'S TIME TO . . .

ZOOGIE

BOOGIE!

They warm up with a **SWING, SWAY, JUMP,** and **JIVE.** They let loose with a **WIGGLE, SQUIGGLE.** Oh, how they **JIGGLE.**

There are **NO RULES.**

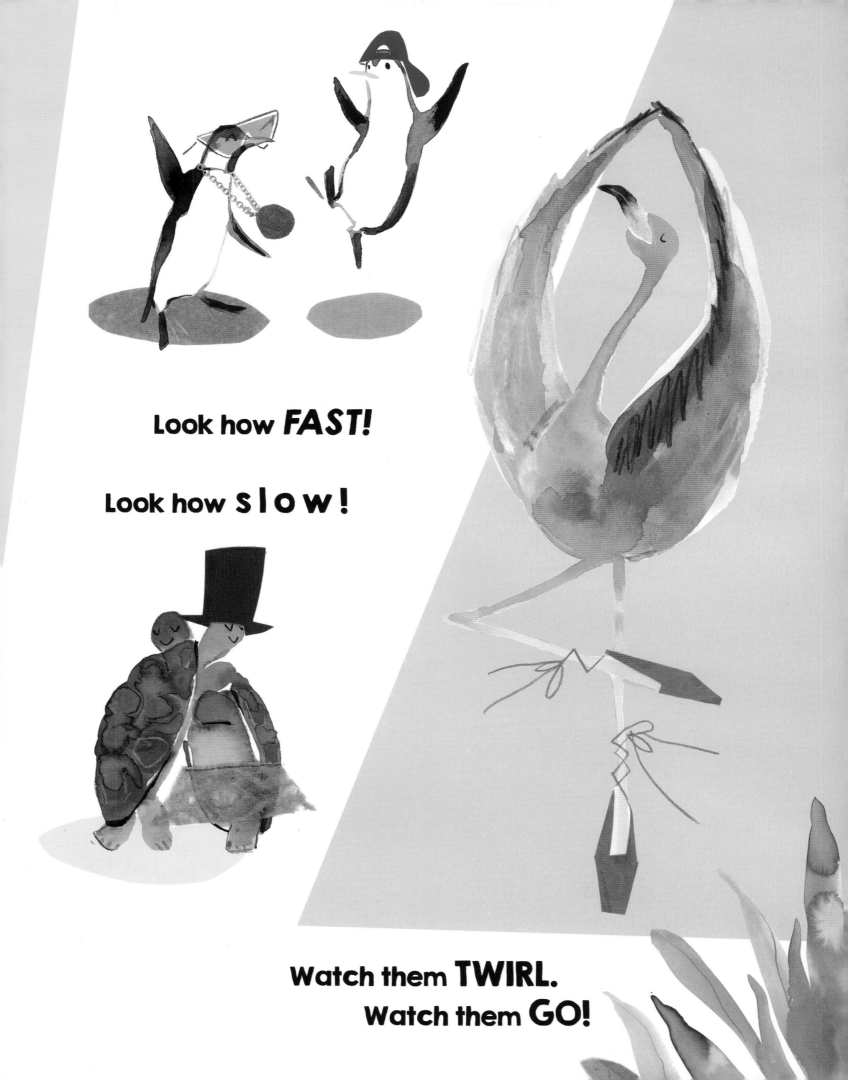

Look how **FAST!**

Look how slow!

Watch them **TWIRL.**
Watch them **GO!**

Some moves have names,
some do **NOT.**

That's the
"TANGO,"

and there's the
"FOX-TROT."

I'll let YOU guess what **THAT'S** called!

But wait. **UH-OH!**
Someone's coming!
What are they going to . . .

PHEW!
That was close.
Maybe they
shouldn't be so . . .

...WILD!

But they can't stop **MOVING** . . .
just look at them **GROOVING!**

Watch those **FURRY FEET** . . .
dance to their own **FUNKY BEAT!**

Some shake their
tails and get
HIP-HOP HAPPY.

Others spread their
wings and go all
FEATHER FLAPPY.

They're not always so **untamed.**
When the dance mood is **right** . . .

every **night,** they line up in **files . . .**
clearing the **aisles** to really get down and . . .

Samba, salsa, **cha-cha-cha.**
Mambo, polka, **pop and lock.**

You ask, when will they ever **stop?**

Well, don't tell a **SOUL,**
but those **PARTY ANIMALS . . .**

they **ZOOGIE BOOGIE**
well into the **NIGHT.**

They **BOOGIE WOOGIE**
with all their **MIGHT** until dawn . . .

Just in time for the **ZOO** to open and they can finally get some Zzzzzzzzs. Sheesh! I'm pooped too.

Let's go get some rest in this morning light so we can strut our stuff with these animals tonight. But remember . . .

DON'T. TELL. ANYONE.